INTERNATIONAL LOVE

DARCY RAY

THE SOUND of the gavel connecting with the judge's podium has to be the most beautiful sound I've ever heard. With a wide smile, I grab my suitcase full of evidence and nod at the witty gray-haired judge, who looks at me in bewilderment. Now if you'd excuse me, I have a last name to change." With a wink, I exit the court-room with an extra pep to my step and the soft chuckle of the judge echoing in the shocked room.

After five years of insufferable family dinners, a nagging mother-in-law, and increasingly fattening husband, I am free. No more Mrs. Patterson, because, as of thirty seconds ago, I won the case for my divorce and acquired all of his assets. That's what the bastard gets. Cheating on me for four years wasn't enough—no, he had to go ahead and steal the family jewels I inherited and give them to his mistress too. I would have never known about the affair if I hadn't stopped by his office that day. His secretary smugly flashed the jewelry at me, and when I questioned her, she laughed and attempted to wave me away, all while having a blase attitude about the whole confrontation.

Determined to confront the bastard about his infi-delity, I stormed into his office causing the thick wooden doors to slam against the walls, making him jump from his reclined position. His widened eyes glanced at me and quickly darted over my shoulder to his mistress who is babbling on about how I can't just barge in. But before she can mouth anything else, she froze. Scoffing, I rolled my eyes at my husband and stormed out of the office, leaving his mistress to deal with the fact his pants were to his knees with his dick standing all shiny from the little blonde girl who is peeking out from under the desk.

At first, thinking of all the time I had wasted with him while he had an affair enraged me, but then I had realized that this was my escape. Our marriage was love-less and everything about it held me back from achieving my dreams. So over the next couple of days, I had gath-ered every email, text, call log, and credit card transaction possible. With all that in hand, I contacted my girlfriend, who happens to be a well-known lawyer, and got her on the case.

Wanting to completely erase him from my life for good, I stop by the receptionist's desk and pay an extra fee to leave with the documentation to change my name. With the freshly printed paper hot in my hands, I strut to my blue bimmer and haul ass to the social security office. It only takes me a few minutes to get to the old-school brick building, and thankfully, there is parking right in front.

Popping down the visor, I give myself a once-over, making sure to fluff my thick sandy-blonde waves and wipe away any rogue lipstick smudges. Sliding out of my car, I pull my pale-pink button-up corduroy skirt down.

Even with thicker thighs that constantly touch, the skirt always finds a way to ride up, making the brown marble buttons that hold it together bunch up. It only takes a few wiggles, and everything slides back into place . . . barely. The girls are barely covered up by a baby-pink lace body-suit with thin straps and a neckline that accentuates them more than needed. So, wiggling around is mighty precarious.

Satisfied that I won't catch a charge from my outfit alone, I grab my prized paper and lock up the bimmer. The steady clicking of my heels on the concrete and the lively chirping of the birds draw me into a calm place mentally, but that's quickly shattered when I walk into the Social Security Administration. Skidding to a stop, I gape at the number of people crowding the small waiting room—nearly forty people consisting of teenagers fiddling on their cells, mothers soothing their teething babies, and old men with sweaty pits.

Arching a brow, I make my way over to the front desk to receive my number in the queue. The old biddy behind the desk is vigorously tapping away at the keyboard with her tongue peeking out of the side of her mouth. Her curls that were probably prim and proper this morning are poufed out and wild. Not wanting to disturb her obviously serious work, I prop my elbows on the counter and gently smile down at her.

"I'll be with you in just a sec, darling." With a few more taps to her worn keyboard, she gives a satisfied nod and spins to face me. "What can I help you w—" Her jaw drops as she takes me in from head to toe. Her lips pucker with distaste and her shoulders stiffen. "What can I do for you?"

Now usually, I would be snippy and call her out on her snap judgment based upon my appearance, but something about her is making me hesitate. Cocking my head to the side, I take in her secretary-like skirt suit, her oversized pearl earrings, and the three shades too light skin complexion where a ring used to sit. "I get it, Ms. Jones, you don't like how I dress or my bold makeup, but I'm willing to bet it's not because you think I'm exposing too much. I bet it's because, as a young gal, you lived wildly and became the true trollop of the town but then you met the one. You know, the soldier who just joined Uncle Sam and was signed up to go overseas soon. Not wanting to pass it up, you got hitched and fell into domestic bliss without any complaints. But what they don't know is every now and then, you would line your lipstick a little brighter than normal, and the charcoal liner would be just a smidgen thicker—it gave you a hint of the old life. Years went by, and no one questioned it, but now the one is no longer with you, and you feel robbed of all the fun you coulda had." Pausing, I let my words sink in and watch the range of emotions play out on her face. "Now, Ms. Jones, tell me, am I wrong?"

Her cheeks flush to the brightest shade of red I think I've ever seen, and after a few sputtered words, she subtly shakes her head. After clearing her throat, she looks to me once again and mumbles, "How could you possibly know all that?"

Chuckling, I tap the counter with my freshly done

baby pink acrylic nails and grab my wallet. "Let me give you a card to a lady who has been helping me. When you call, just say Royal referred you, and they will understand, and if anything, maybe we can have lunch sometime to compare notes." Sliding a matte black card out, I grab a pen and scribble my cell on the back. With the logo facing down, I slide it over to her. Hesitantly, she takes the card and looks it over. I see her eyes reread the front a couple of times, and when it clicks, she looks at me with wide, shiny eyes.

Tucking the card into her coat pocket, she straightens in her seat and peers behind me at the line forming. "What are you here for, ma'am?" This time when she asks, it's with a whole new attitude.

"I'm here to make my divorce official. I need my name changed." With a sweet smile, she nods and activates the machine that spits out my number. With the little paper in hand, I saunter over to an empty seat and make myself comfortable.

Surprisingly my number is called mighty quick. I look suspiciously over to Ms. Jones, and sure enough, she gives me a wink and a smile. I guess being as observant as I am, has its perks.

IT'S BEEN six weeks since getting my new lease on life, and every day is a new adventure, but even with the new adventures, I can't escape the nagging feeling that I'm missing something. Flopping back on my sectional couch, I look out the floor-to-ceiling windows overlooking the Mississippi River and watch as a plane leaves a puffy white trail in its wake. On the seat beside me, my phone starts going crazy with notifications.

Unwillingly, I scoop up the annoying device and do a quick scroll to see if it's anything important.

I should have known who it is. I've been avoiding my mother, who's been texting and calling me nonstop. After our last conversation about how I'm ruining the family name and how leaving my husband was the worst mistake I could ever make, I've decided not to answer until she apologizes. Which, let's face it, will probably be over her dead body.

Fatigued from the morning's Zumba session, I gather myself and amble along to my bed. "Gah, why do you have to be in my way? Can't you see I just want to flop onto my comfy bed without having to move anything?" I don't even know why I try, it's not like my purse is going to talk back. Good thing no one is here to see me because they would have me locked in the looney bin for sure. I mean, seriously, who talks to their purse?

Grumbling, I grab the handle of my Dooney and Bourke purse to move it to the floor, but one handle slips from my grasp, causing all the contents to spill onto the floor. If two-year-old me could see me now, she would be shocked at how well I can throw a temper tantrum—with my little feet stomps, the way I throw my head back, moaning and groaning because of the inconvenience.

Luckily I'm an adult, so I don't have to pick up my mess. Instead, I push everything to the floor and collapse onto my king-sized bed, by the pastel-pink down comforter engulfing me. Rolling over, I start to wiggle my way under the duvet, but as I move, something hot pink catches my eye. Reaching down, I grab the item and bring it into view. My passport. Something I've never used. I got it to travel the world with the person I thought was the love of my life.

Sitting upright with the passport in hand, I struggle with the blankets wrapped around my legs and fall to the ground. As I scramble to my feet, my long locks decide to fly over my head and cover my eyes. With one big hair flip, I sling them back to their proper place, slip on a tube of lipstick, and fly back onto the bed. "Stupid lipstick! Get out of my way! I got shit to do!" Jumping back out of bed, this time avoiding the killer lipstick, I nearly run to my desk and pry my laptop open.

My legs bounce in anticipation as the laptop starts, and no matter how advanced my Mac is or how fast my internet speed is, everything seems to be running slower than I need. Finally, the home screen pops up, and after a few clicks, taps, and scrolls, I click submit. "I can't believe I just did that." Wide-eyed, I look over to my supersized unicorn, who is staring right back at me. "I just bought a ticket to London, Francis. I'm leaving tonight!"

Realization of what I just did hits me as soon as the words are out of my mouth. My heart starts racing as I think about everything I need to do before I can get onto the flight. "Focus, Royal! Now that you're divorced, you need to go out there and live your best life. You can do this!" After my little pep talk, I take a few deep breaths and begin to think logically. "Right! First things first, Francis! Reserve a place to stay for my trip and make a quick itinerary. After that, pack." Looking over to my closet, I realize the daunting task ahead of me. Turning back towards my fluffy unicorn with wide eyes, I utter, "I think we are going to need more suitcases, Francis."

Nearly six hours later, I have all my ducks in a row and all my luggage in tow. Since I took my ex for everything he was worth in the divorce, I got a first-class seat on the flight and all the room one could possibly need. "This is your captain speaking, we are preparing for take-off. Please remain in your seats until indicated." Sure enough, the plane begins its trek down the runway, and as my turmoil gets further and further away, the more excited I become about this adventure. "Daddy ain't raise no bitch!"

"LADIES AND GENTLEMEN, we have arrived at London Heathrow airport, please be patient with your departure and ensure you do not forget any belongings you might have missed before departing. Again, Thank you for flying Coastal Airlines, Captain out." Hearing the captain's strained voice makes me so grateful that I'm not the one flying, and more appreciative of the nap I took for nearly the whole flight. With a snap, I undo my belt buckle and stand to retrieve my carry-on luggage. As I pull my tote down, my small travel-sized shampoos start spilling out of the side pocket. "Oh, snickerdoodle!" Dropping the bag into the chair, I squat down and start blindly searching under the seat for my supplies. That is until a manly hand bumps into mine, startling me. Yanking my hand back, I snap upright and look up to see who the mysterious hand belongs to. Boy, am I surprised to see a tall, broad-shouldered, muscular-armed man with bourbon-colored hair and matching beard, eyes sweeter than honey, and two dimples that would drive any woman crazy. "Oh, I'm . . . I'm so sorry, I'm such a klutz!"

If I thought he was sexy with just dimples, I'm terribly wrong. When his plush lips spread into a sinful grin, I nearly cream myself. "No worries, love." Extending his hand, he holds the two bottles that escaped their confinement. "I rescued these for you. Can't have a pretty lady like yourself going without." His sweet words set my cheeks aflame, and if I would have fanned myself, I know it would only make me hotter.

"Why, thank you, good sir. I must have forgotten to zip the pocket back up." Being the little southern belle that I am, I can't help but lay the accent on thick. I start to ask the sexier-than-sin specimen in front of me a question, but the loud clearing of a throat cuts me off. Looking over his shoulder, I see a line of impatient passengers waiting to disembark. "Silly me, let me get out of y'all's way." Shoving the bottles into the bag, I quickly close it and step into the aisle to exit the plane.

I make it through the airport with surprisingly little difficulty, and just as I start to exit through the revolving doors, someone taps me on the shoulder. Spinning around, I come chest to chest with the glorious man from the plane. "Oh, pardon me. Can I help you?"

Chuckling, he tilts his chin towards the door and says, "I assume you haven't been here before. Am I right?"

Following his gaze, I watch the people walking out the door wearing heavy coats and then look down at my own attire of black leggings and an oversized baby-blue sweater. Frowning, I move my gaze back to Mr. Sexy and shrug one shoulder. "I guess I gotta freeze my tokus off until I can catch a cab to my hotel." Maybe some chilly weather will cool me enough until I can get to my vibrator because this man is giving my panties a run for their money.

With that glorious knee-weakening smile, he chuckles and slips his topcoat off his shoulders and drapes it over mine. I'm instantly warmed up, but I'm not sure if it's from the thickly-lined coat or his thumbs sliding along my collar bone. As they move along my freckled skin, he dips beneath my sweater, causing a shiver that I know he sees. "I can't possibly fathom an exquisite goddess such as yourself being anything less than warm in the bitter conditions outside."

"Oh, I can't possibly take your coat! I—" His long thin finger pressing against my full lips cuts me off mid-sentence. Batting my lashes, I slowly close my mouth, sliding my lips against his finger that looks as if he could work the keys of the grandest piano. It takes everything I have to stop myself from sliding his fingers deep into my mouth and sucking, imagining that it was his cock.

With hooded eyes, he brushes his finger softly against my lips before pulling it away and swallows deeply, making his Adam's apple bob. "You wouldn't happen to be staying at Park Plaza, would you?"

"Why, yes, I am." I've never been so thankful for my padded bra because with the sexual vibes flying around on the crisp cool breeze, I feel like my nipples could cut diamonds. When his eyes dart down to my pert breasts, I start to feel as if he can see right through the tulle and silk barrier.

"Well, I think fate worked its magic just right. I happen to be staying there as well. I insist you take the coat, and we can discuss returning it when we've arrived at the hotel." Not bothering to hear any of my sputtering objections, he holds his arm out for me, grabs the handle of my luggage, and escorts me to the curb where we hail a cab together.

OUR CAB RIDE to the hotel couldn't have been any tenser, and when I say tense, I mean sexually. It took everything I had to stop myself from rubbing my thighs together, at the same time, I had to make sure my legs were together because my desire for this stranger was potent, leaving my panties drenched and done for. For the whole ride, I either stared out the window or looked down at my feet . . . all to avoid the glances from the driver in the rearview mirror and the subtle deep breaths I caught Mr. Sexy doing out of the corner of my eye. Every once in awhile, I would see him look me up and down while biting his bottom lip or stretching his hand as if he was restraining himself from touching me.

As soon as we make it to our hotel, I pay the driver while Mr. Sexy tips, and then we grab our bags. I reach into the trunk to retrieve my carry-on duffel bag, and when I do, I hear a groan from behind me, followed by a cough in an attempt to cover it up. You know what, I hopped on that plane to have an adventure, why can't that include hot sex with a sexy foreigner? Set on my plan, I grab my bag and lean out from the trunk, giving Mr. Sexy a wink as I walk into the hotel.

I'm nearly done checking in by the time he joins me

at the front desk, and as he approaches, the receptionist looks over to him with a friendly smile, "Good evening, Mr. Foster, I hope your trip was successful."

"Ah, Janice, I'm glad to see you back at work, I assume you had a refreshing vacation?"

Janice's cheeks burn as she dips her head and nods. "Yes sir, I did, thank you." Taking a deep breath, she puts her professional face back on and continues, "Will you be staying with us for the usual?"

Mr. Foster, the sexy specimen that affects my libido—and Janice's—openly devours my curves with his eyes and looks to me. "How long are you staying for, my lady?"

Turning her lustful gaze from Mr. Foster to me, Janice stutters and begins to apologize, "I'm sorry about that, ma'am. Let me finish checking you in, and for the inconvenience, I will add a complimentary bottle of our finest wine."

"Oh, just call me Royal, and I completely understand. Mr. Foster is a delicious treat for the eyes but pure torture for our ladybits." Both Janice and Mr. Foster sputter at my bold choice of words, causing me to chuckle.

Pushing from the counter, Mr. Foster steps to my side, closing the distance between us. With him standing in such close proximity, I have to look up to see his eyes that burn with intensity. "Hmm, I quite like that name, Royal. It fits you." The way my name rolls off his tongue sends shivers down my spine. The urge to have him shouting my name as I ride his perfect body, grinding my clit against his pelvis while he cums inside of me over-takes my mind causing my cheeks to pink again.

His fingers trailing over the side of my face pull me from my lustful thoughts, and when I break through the sex haze clouding my vision, I see his sinful grin staring down at me. "You can call me Ramsay, and trust me when I say I'm not one for torture, but keep in mind that the line between pain and pleasure is one I like dabbling with."

"Ohh, I think you're gonna have to show me that line." With my bottom lip tucked between my teeth, I rise onto my toes until I'm a hair's breadth away from his pillowy lips. My mind is so focused on claiming his very kissable mouth, but yet again, the sound of someone clearing their throat yanks me back to reality.

Pursing my lips, I look towards the receptionist who is fumbling her hands while looking between Ramsay and me and then over my shoulder. Following her gaze, I see the disgruntled frown on the shrew's face. "You're really taking the biscuit there, aren't ya? Don't be so daft, we don't want to see that hanky-panky here." Her accent is rich and a surprise to me, and even though I know she's being pissy, I can't help but snicker at myself for being chided.

"Bless your heart, ma'am, I didn't mean to be rude. I just couldn't contain my love for this man any longer. After all, I'm practically his mail-order bride." Even though I know my words are nothing but a fib, butterflies still erupt in my stomach, making me feel giddy. Just as I expected, the shrew gasps in horror and grabs her blouse as if pulling it closed will save her.

To my surprise, Ramsay wraps his arm around my waist, pulling me closer so that my pebbled nipples press against his firm chest and bends so that as he talks, puffs of air blow against the back of my ear. "Come, my love, we can begin our honeymoon in our hotel room where there will be no interruptions." With a mind of its own, my body arches up against him, causing me to fight the urge to moan from all the sweet sensations of his taut body and the bulge from his erection pressing into me.

SMACK!

Purely sinful pain registers in my brain, and just as fast it's gone, shooting down to my core and changing into pure desire. Shocked, I look wide-eyed to Ramsay, whose hooded eyes and crooked grin show he knows the effect that the spanking had on me. "Grab your stuff, and let's go." The fire licking in my veins ignites into an inferno with the command in his words.

Without hesitating, I grab my keycard and my bags—all while ignoring the cherry-faced receptionist and old bitty, both of which are both staring at us in horror. With everything in hand, we speed walk to the elevator, which is already open thanks to the liftman fighting to hide his knowing grin. Pressed against the mahogany wall, I watch Ramsay press the floor number and clasp his hands behind his back, patiently waiting for the door to slide closed. Everything about him screams calm and in control, yet I can barely contain the thrill and lust coursing through me, shooting down to my throbbing pussy. Even when I first got with my ex-husband, our sex life was never as exciting as this; and Ramsay and I haven't even done anything. I've lived vicariously through my charity functions and books, but now I finally have the chance to partake in the exhilarating experience.

As the doors finally close, I half expect him to jump on me like you see in the movies, but instead, he stands facing the door without giving me any indication that he is serious about what he said and the meaning of his actions. Confused by his silence, I fight off the urge to run my hands over his firm body and begin to stomp the raging fire in my veins down. By the time the door to the elevator opens again, I have my mindset on pulling out the good ol' vibrator to ease the burn, and a plan to enjoy my week in London to erase Ramsay from my mind.

Fortunately for me, my room is on the same floor as his, so instead of following him, I start to follow the signs that point me where to go. "Royal, where are you going?" Ramsay's words make me pause, and when I turn to look at him, I startle because he's closed the distance between us and is once again towering over me.

"Excuse me, sir, but I'm not here to play games. I'm always down for a good fuck, but leading me on is not kosher." I try to remain proper, but it's been a long day, and walking around with a throbbing core and drenched panties are not my idea of comfort.

"Leading you on? Oh, beautiful, you are gravely mistaken. See, there are cameras in that elevator, and as much as I fancy a snog in front of an audience, anything more intimate than that will happen in the confines of privacy. Now, be a good girl and take your sweet, round behind to my room." My channel clenches from the tone of his command and the tender spot on my rear throbs, reminding me of the delicious pain awaiting me.

With my mind made up, I flip my thick, unruly hair over my shoulder and follow him into the unknown.

After years of nothing but plain vanilla sex, I thought calling someone Daddy and spanking in the bedroom only happened in books. Reading about it on my Kindle is nothing compared to the mind-blowing sex marathon I had with Ramsay. Our one night stand ended up turning into a full week together—full of sightseeing in the beautiful town, trying new food, and of course, exploring all kinds of new things. As much as I wish I could have extended my stay, I already had another flight booked and waiting for me, so with a promise to keep in touch, I boarded a jet heading to my next destination. Ireland.

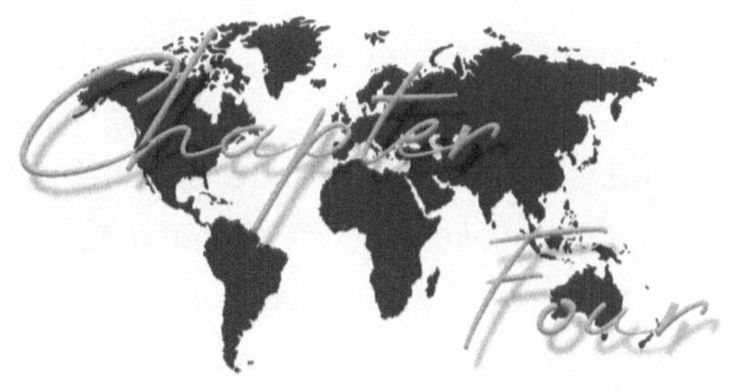

I'VE BEEN IN GALWAY, Ireland for three days already, and I swear it's the most beautiful place I've ever seen. Between the rolling hills and iconic cliffs overlooking the bay, I could stay here forever. That is if I didn't already have a life back in the States and the fact that my hair just doesn't get along with the weather. Rain and humidity be damned. Like today, for instance, I'm supposed to be taking the bus to Dublin to explore the famous city, but the torrential downpour has put a halt to my plans. Now, I plan on drowning myself in authentic Irish stew and the darkest ale at the quaint pub near my Airbnb.

With it being midday, you'd figure it would only be me, the barkeep, and some crickets, but when I walk in, I skid to a stop from the jam-packed pub. Looking around, I take in the genuine smiles and hearty laughter mixing with the clinking of silverware against plates. The warmth that radiates from everyone instantly fills me with acceptance, unlike the cold and distant diners in the States. Unfortunately, all the tables are occupied, but as I turn to leave, I see a gorgeous redhead waving in my direction. Just to make sure he's looking at me, I point to myself in confirmation, and with a smile, he nods his head.

Not wanting to ruin my adventurous streak, I shrug my shoulders and make my way through the crowded room. In the dim light, I can't make out much more than his short, tousled red hair and the matching stubble from his way-after-five o'clock shadow, but the closer I get to him, the more I want to skip stew and go straight for dessert. Hiding underneath his stubble are dimples that deepen the more his smile widens, and thanks to the single ray of light shining in his eyes, I can see the pale-blue swirls that trace down my curves as I approach.

He rises from his chair and stands by the empty one in front of his. "Mind eating lunch with me?" His question catches me by surprise, but with only a small falter in my steps, I close the distance and sit in the chair that he pulls out for me.

"Thank you for allowing me to sit with you, I was starting to think I was gonna miss out on the pub's famous stew. "

"'Tis nothing. I couldn't see myself passing up an opportunity to eat with such a beauty." His thick, burly accent curls around me in such a poetic way, making all my second guesses disappear as I settle into the chair.

"Why ain't you a charmer? I bet you say that to all the ladies around here, and with how delicious you look, I can't even fathom you being cold at night." My bold assumption makes him nearly choke on the amber ale in his cup, causing a drop to slip past his lips and trail down his chin. The bead of moisture catches my attention, making it so I can't help but watch it cling to the edge of his chin, threatening to fall. As it hangs with all its might, my mind starts imaging the naughtiest things—the drop turns from ale to my sweet nectar, and instead of speaking gorgeous words, his mouth will write poetry over my throbbing nub as I wiggle beneath his hands.

My raging hormones send a wave of desire through my channel that begs to be filled. I used to be able to go months without having sex, but Ramsay ruined that for me. Now all I want to do is fly back to London, or wherever he is, and become his slave in bed once again. and have him warm my butt cheeks with his strong hands. All it would take is a single text, and I would be on a plane there, but I can't. This trip is for me to find myself, and getting hooked on the first person I spread my legs for won't help.

Clearing my throat, I look back into the swirling blues that are now bloodshot from choking. With a devilish grin, he takes another swig of his ale, this time emptying the tankard. When he's swallowed it all down, he says, "You, lass, are something else. I'm not one to be shocked easily, but you take the cake on that."

"What can I say, being a repressed housewife with a collection of erotic books has loosened me up a bit, and to be honest, there are no panties to get out of a wad here." Underneath my thick fleece leggings is nothing but bare skin waiting to be marked by hands and reddened from spankings. If not for my long hair being draped over my shoulders, you would see my pebbled nipples are rubbing erotically against the soft material of my shirt, making me happily uncomfortable.

"By gods, they have heard my prayers and bestowed me with a queen. What's ye' name, you vixen?"

"Royal. Royal Rockefeller. What about you? Or should I presume the legends are true, and you are Satan's spawn?"

"You can call me Finley if you prefer, but according to the other lasses that warm my sheets as you say, they prefer to call me God."

"You're living up to the stereotype, aren't yah, redhead? I hope you have something to back all that up with."

"Oh, I got something that's mighty cocky, but you, lass, are just gonna have to wait to see for yourself. I may be fighting a raging dick that wants to be buried in your sassy mouth, but I am a gentleman. So let's get you some stew and our famous ale in your belly first." With a wave of his hand, he signals for the server to come over and then turns back to me with hooded eyes and a predatory glare. I'm going to be ruined, and I don't even care.

Needing to alleviate my throbbing nub, I cross my legs and subtly start rubbing them together. Seeing the change in my position, Finley smirks and reaches under the table to adjust himself. Our silent dance to become comfortable fails, and the longer we simmer in our lustful glances, the more it becomes a race to see who can withstand pulling the other to the bathroom to have their way.

Luckily our server returns with two tankards brimming with dark ale and a steaming bowl of Irish stew, giving us something to focus on instead of each other.

SCATTERED atop our table are numerous emptied tankards laying askew. I tried keeping track of how many there were, but somewhere between the chugging competitions and hilarious arm wrestling, I lost count. My face hurts from smiling so much, and I swear there should be a fire between my thighs from me rubbing them together constantly.

Let's not forget the amount of alcohol coursing through my system, which only makes my aching need worse. I had hoped the stew would absorb the potency, but much to my dismay, it didn't.

So here I am, two sheets to the wind with my hair in disarray, eyeing the hall that leads to the bathroom as I try to calculate the chances of us getting caught doing the dirty.

With how jumbled my thoughts are, I find it hilarious that I'm even attempting to calculate because every time my mind comes up with the same answer: yes!

Leaning across the table, Finley taps my arm and whispers, "Psst."

"Hmm?" When I turn towards him, I can't help but snort at how ridiculous he looks. It's like our mission to get laid has become a top-secret assignment, which by the snickers around us, we've already failed.

"I'm going to the bathroom. Wink, wink."

The fact that he actually said "wink, wink" makes me lose it completely. With one arm wrapped around my waist as I full-body laugh, I use my other hand to wave him off, and with hazy eyes, I watch him amble off towards the bathroom and stopping at the bar to hand the barkeep some cash to pay our tab.

When Finley disappears into the darkness, I start getting nervous at the idea of getting caught, and just as I start to back out of it, a large crowd comes through the door cheering and calling for ale. With the servers and barkeep occupied, I gather my courage and slink off after Finley. This is, after all, something I've always wanted to do.

Thankfully there is only one other door back here, and that's the supply closet, so the risk of me walking in on someone else is slim. Not bothering to knock, I slip into the

bathroom door and lock it behind me. I barely have a chance to turn towards Finley before he has me pinned against the door with his mouth over mine and his body grinding against my curves. As soon as I open my mouth to his probing tongue, he slides his hands under my sweater and groans. I can't help but arch into his hands, filling them with my heavy breasts. Not one to miss a beat, Finley drags my pert nipples between his fingers and starts to manipulate them to his will. With a final pinch and swirl, I let out a moan that gets lost in our frantic kissing.

With a pop, Finley pulls his mouth away from mine and slides his hands out from under my sweater and begins to fumble with his jeans. "Fuck, I can't wait anymore, slip out of your clothes, lass. I need to see you bent over the counter with your bare ass in the air."

Using the counter to help balance myself, I quickly kick off my boots and shimmy my leggings down and suck in a breath as the cool air collides with my glistening folds. Bending over, I slip my feet from the narrow holes of my jeans, and when I straighten up, I gasp. "Holy shit, there's no way that's going to fit inside me! No wonder you're so damn cocky!"

When I say big, I mean it. His hands, which are large, working man hands, can barely fit around his shaft. Seeing my shocked look, he chuckles and gives his cock a squeeze, which leaks precum from the tip.

The tone of his voice reminds me of Ramsay and his bossy ways, causing my channel to clench, begging to be filled. Spinning around, I lean over the counter and spread my legs, exposing my pussy that's so drenched it's starting to run down my legs. Through the mirror, I watch as Finley steps closer to me and dips so that he can align his dick with my sheath, but instead of sliding in, he runs his shaft against my folds, nudging my throbbing nub at the same time. Each time he bumps against it, I climb higher and higher but never close enough to reach an orgasm.

After one last thrust through my drenched folds, he

pulls back and presses the head of his cock into my opening, but doesn't slide in any further. I can feel the stretching from just the head, and from what I saw, his dick only gets bigger the further down the shaft you go. In an effort to get in a better position, I adjust my feet which makes me shift against his shaft. The slight movement pushes his cock a little further into my stretching channel, forcing a moan mixed with a pained cry out of me.

"I got you, lass, hold steady." I jump when his deft fingers land on my engorged clit and begin to stroke it in fast circles, quickly erasing the pain and replacing it with glorious euphoria. A mini orgasm explodes from me, relaxing all my muscles, and with a new coat of lubricant soaking my channel, he begins to slowly move his hips, steadily pushing himself deeper inside.

Every inch that slides into me stretches parts of me that I've never felt before, and the urge to have him fuck me silly overwhelms me. Lifting my head, I look back into the mirror to see his head leaned back with his bottom lip tucked between his teeth.

Somewhere between making out to now, he removed his shirt, and the six-pack he had hidden underneath is left exposed for me to ogle. With each thrust, they tighten, and his pleasureful grin turns into one of concentration.

Throwing caution to the wind, I slam back against him as he thrusts, causing him to bottom out. Both of us let out a string of curses, and when the stinging starts to fade, the fullness hits me. In that moment, I lock eyes with him and pant, "Fuck me, Finley! Fuck me like the cocky redhead you are!"

He lets go of all control and gives me exactly what I begged for. Our bodies connect together in a furious fuck session, and with each thrust, the head of his cock slides against the delicate spot deep inside of me. Each tantalizing pump has me clawing at the counter to run from the delicious abuse, and at the same time, my channel clenches like a vice grip to keep the source of my pleasure imprisoned.

It doesn't take Finley long to get into a rhythm, but when he does, it's punishing and unforgiving. All my nerve endings are alive and rapid firing, so when he starts to run his rough hands over the curve of my ass and onto my hips, I have to bite my bottom lip to quiet my moan. I half expect him to redden my bottom with his hand as Ramsay did, but he doesn't. In between the sweet pain and core tightening pounding, a fleeting feeling of disappointment hits me.

Pushing the distracting emotions away, I reach down until my trembling fingers reach my aching clit. The jolt of pleasure is enough to make me forget about the man who's been torturing my dreams for the past couple nights with his icy-blue eyes and devilish grin. Each twirl of my fingers pushes away the thoughts of how Ramsay made me feel like a goddess under his assertive ways. Each pinch pushes away how even though he was dominating my body, I was the one in control, setting the pace that matches my comfort level and how fucking glorious my orgasm was when he finally gave it to me.

Behind me, Finley starts to lose his rhythm, and from

what I learned very well from my prior marriage, he is about to lose his load before even letting me catch mine. Closing my eyes, I focus on the fullness and pulse of pleasure every time he rubs over my soft spot. The tight ball deep in my core swells, and with each thrust, it gets closer and closer to exploding.

I can feel my channel quiver and just as I crest the top . . . someone bangs on the door. "Hey, hurry up, ye shite! Squeeze it off!" Behind me, I hear Finley curse and begin to thrust even harder. Not wanting to be left hanging, I pick up where I left off, bringing myself back to the cusp.

Just as my channel clenches down one last time, Finley stills and lets out a guttural groan, filling me with his cum. Together we fall into a post-orgasmic bliss, breathing in the sweet aroma of sexual essence and soaking in our perspiration caused by the exertion put into reaching that bliss.

As much as I want to lay in his arms for post-coital cuddling, the pounding at the door sounds again. Slipping from my drenched folds, Finley shuffles behind me, followed by the sound of a zipper. "You got you a nice one, lass, better than most. You might want to wipe up, I unloaded quite a bit." With a smack to my thigh, I watch as he slips out the bathroom leaving me bent over the bathroom sink with cum running down my thigh and an instant realization that just because he knew how to work his big dick, doesn't mean he isn't a fucking dick.

With some wet toilet paper, I wipe myself up as much as I can and slide my leggings back on. Giving myself a once over in the mirror, I pause and sigh in disappointment. "Dammit, Royal, stop feeling sorry for yourself. Not all sexual experiences are going to be as amazing as when you were with Ramsay." Rolling my eyes, I fluff my overly thick waves and walk out of the scene of a great, yet unsatisfying sexual encounter.

I COULDN'T BE MORE ready to leave Ireland. After being left to fend for myself, I not only have to do the walk of shame out of the bathroom with nearly everyone in the pub watching me with a knowing look, but the whole way back to my Airbnb, I got rained on which turned me into a soggy mess. Thanks to my obviously different style, news spread around about my escapade making me a target for pointy fingers and snickers, so I spent the rest of the trip cooped up.

But when I say cooped up, I mean browsing through multiple different tropes of porn while breaking in my new dildo with a suctioning bud that stimulates my clit. The magical device not only made me combust in six seconds flat, but after the sexually fueled video chat with Daddy, I couldn't even bring myself to move from the puddle caused by the much-needed orgasm. There's something erotic about being told what to do as I pleasure myself and even with him being over a thousand miles away, I felt as if he was the one controlling my pleasure— from the rate that the phallic device thrust into my squelching pussy and the speed of the vibrations that sent my inner nerve endings into overdrive.

Even with the mind-blowing video sex, I couldn't bring

myself to go out on my last night here. Instead, I spent the night packing my suitcases on wobbly legs, so that as soon as the sun blesses me with its presence, I could skedaddle. Now here I am, sitting at the airport with a steaming cup of Starbucks coffee with nearly four hours until boarding starts, staring at my phone. It's taken me three times to reread what Daddy just commanded me to do.

Daddy: Go to the bathroom, slip your panties off, and send me a picture of that glistening pussy.

My cheeks redden at his vulgar words. There's something about reading commands instead of hearing them, it's like they are written in stone with no way to pretend you didn't hear him or run away. No, the words are encrypted in my cell phone that is connected with towers sending signals across the world.

Royal: But Daddy, I'm at the airport.

Daddy: That's how bad girls get spanked. You have until the count of three.

Royal: Now who's being a brat.

Daddy: One

Daddy: Two

Anticipation grips me, making my heart flutter against my chest at the thought of getting punished. I've had a sample of what it's like to be a bad girl when Ramsay is in control, and though he lavished attention and care on me afterward, I made sure to be on my best behavior. Fumbling with my phone, I quickly reply and look for the nearest bathroom.

*Royal: *pouts* Fiiinnee, you win.*

Daddy: Oh, while you're at it, toss your panties. I want as few barriers between your pussy and my cock as possible.

I'm twenty-eight, and , and I've read some books that would make my great twice-removed grandmother roll over in her grave. With flaming cheeks, I shuffle to the bathroom closest to my gate. Claiming the big stall, I quickly lock the door and begin to pace around. "Deep breaths, Royal, it's only the airport, where thousands of people walk every day, from all over the world." Stomping my foot, I look down at my black leggings and nearly screech from anxiety. "I signed up for this when I hopped on that plane to London, now stop being a chicken! It's not like people can see through your leggings."

The sound of my phone dinging makes me instinctively clench my ass to prepare for the spanking, but when it doesn't happen, a tinge of sadness hits me. In this defining moment, I finally accept that vanilla sex will never be for me, and thanks to Ramsay, I've gotten a chance to dip my fingers into the kink pool. I have a feeling I've only just skimmed the surface.

With my mind made up, I hook my thumbs into both my leggings and lace thong and slide them down in one fluid movement. After a couple of stumbles and multiple pictures later, I do as Daddy demanded and send him the picture that he wanted; a snapshot of my glistening pussy and discarded panties.

Daddy: There's my kitten, with perfectly smiling lips

begging me to dip my tongue in between to lap at the sweet juices.

Royal: Did I please you, Daddy?

Daddy: Yes, princess, now get dressed and enjoy your flight, I must return to my meeting.

Just like that, I'm left with an aching core that is begging to be filled with Daddy's cock—to help ease my sexual frustration that a toy can't even touch. To make matters worse, the seam of my leggings presses against my sensitive clit, and with every step or movement, it rubs, only making the situation worse. I bet this is punishment for making him wait.

THE FLIGHT to my next destination couldn't have been any more uncomfortable, and my unease must've been evident because the poor attendants kept offering me little glasses of wine. Little do they know, the wine was only causing the situation to worsen. I was half tempted to reach into my carry-on bag and snag my pocket vibrator to induct myself into my self-made Mile High Club, but the fear of an attendant catching me changed my mind.

My FLIGHT to France took just under two hours, leaving me plenty of time to grab a bite to eat and settle in for the day. With a quick refresher to my voluptuous hair, I head to the front desk to get some recommendations, and lucky for me, she is quite helpful. So here I am, standing in front of a small black-brick mom-and-pop diner that has one single trifold sign that lists the special of the day. Ivy clings to the brick, weaving through the cracks, forming an intricate natural design. Outside are four small metal tables that seat two to three people.

. . .

STEPPING THROUGH THE DOOR, I take my time to soak in the atmosphere that exudes dark and dangerous, yet comforting all at the same time. Pictures of brightly painted nude women and men are scattered amongst the nearly matte walls, delicate plants are strategically placed, and wooden beams line the ceiling. As if the interior wasn't attractive enough, a sweet smell creeps into my nose, luring me to the counter where a freshly baked Parisian Flan sits begging to be eaten. My mouth waters at the sight of the caramelized sugar topping it, making the top layer a delicious deep golden brown.

"WHAT CAN I do for you, mademoiselle?" A sultry voice pulls me from the food porn happening in my head, and when I turn to the source, I nearly choke on the pool of saliva in my mouth. Standing behind the register is Adonis himself, dressed in a black sleeveless shirt that exposes the tattoos covering both arms, black denim skinny jeans, and black combat boots adorned with silver chains. His dirty blond hair hangs down to his chin in a shag, only defining his chiseled features and accentuating his golden eyes.

EMBARRASSED, I quickly swipe at my chin to hide any possible drool and clear my throat to reply. "Oh, sorry, I'm not from here, so if you could surprise me, just include a slice of the piece of heaven you have right there."

Running his hand through shaggy hair, he bites his bottom lip to retain a chuckle and runs his eyes up and down my aching body. "Certainly, can I get you anything else?"

SOMETHING about his devilish grin and the baritone of his voice reminds me of the commands from Ramsay and the feeling of being controlled. The urge to discover more about my sexual fantasies stands at the forefront of my mind wearing only a pink lace nightie. "Actually, do you happen to know any clubs around here that cater to . . . well, cater to the darker desires?"

THE GOLDEN SWIRL in his eyes flares with understanding. Without saying a word, he reaches into his wallet and extracts a business card, holding it just out of reach. "You be a good girl and finish all your food, and I'll give you this card." At his words, the urge to obey overtakes me.

DIPPING MY CHIN, I look through my lashes and coyly say, "Yes, sir." With a nod of his head, he rings me up for my meal and motions for me to have a seat. Reality hits me right on the ass when I remember I'm at a public diner, but when I turn, the few patrons that are scattered throughout the quaint eating area aren't paying me any mind. With a sigh of relief, I claim my table and wait for my much-earned meal.

I MUST HAVE BEEN HUNGRIER than I thought because I quickly devoured the freshly made summer tomato bouil-labaisse and the slice of flan, leaving me overstuffed and grateful the creator of leggings made them stretchy. Sliding back from the table, I start to stand, but a hand lands on my shoulder and pushes me back down. Looking over to the hand, I see swirls of black and red ink making an intricate design that would be mesmerizing to look at, if not for the fact I don't know who it belongs to besides the fact it's a male.

HIS HAND TRAILS up my neck slowly, stopping, so his deft fingers come to rest against my carotid artery. My lips part from the quaking feeling in my core as he begins to steadily press down, giving me only a show of what he could do to me. Only a few seconds later, the pressure is gone, and his hand continues its path, but this time it moves further back and slips underneath the thick wall of hair.

NOT WANTING the foreign sensations to stop, I tilt my head to the side, giving him better access to continue the delicious torture. The hair on my arms stands as he begins to spread his fingers at the base of my skull, and ever so gently, he slides the rest of the way up and curls his hand into a fist with my hair trapped in his grip. Slowly, he begins to pull, creating euphoria that ignites my blood with a desire to be dominated.

As the pressure grows, I'm forced to tilt my head back to look into the eyes of my teaser, and the person I see makes me bite my bottom lip in delight. His molten gold eyes bore into me as if he can read my every want and desire. With him being so close, I can't stop the fluttering of my lashes as I'm overwhelmed by his intoxicating scent.

"You've been a good girl so I'll reward you with what you want. However, the only way to read the card is with a blacklight, so you might want to invest in one." With the hold on my hair released, he bends over my shoulder so that his mouth is beside my ear and whispers, "*J'espère avoir la chance de vous plaire ce soir. Tu es comme une déesse.*" The way his French accent rolls off his tongue and caresses my ear makes me wish his mouth was between my legs so that my pussy can be lavished with such finesse, but before I can ask him what he said, he leaves the card and walks away.

UNDERNEATH MY SUEDE TRENCH COAT, there is nothing but an intricate see-through strappy black lace bralette with a peek-a-boo that shows the inner curve of my breast as it slides to the satin skin underneath, a matching thong, all topped off with a garter belt. The whole time I was getting dressed and applying my warrior paint, I had to remind myself that I set off on this trip for self-discovery, little did I know fate would lead me to the looming building that blends into the night. Taking a deep breath in, I close the distance to the door and step into the next part of my adventure.

From the things I've read in romance books, I've armed myself with some type of knowledge of what to expect, but as I cross the barrier, I'm shocked to see I was led wrong. Instead of a scantily dressed woman parading around or thugs loitering the front door, I am greeted with a bulky security guard who asks for the passcode. After sliding him the card, he makes me sign a waiver, takes my coat, and allows me to pass through. Without my coat to protect me from the unknown, I wrap my arms over myself to provide some sort of barrier, but what I see when I step into the actual club makes me drop my arms and gasp in awe.

The further I walk into the club, the more I become entranced, and with my focus on everything else but what is directly around me, I don't notice the dark silhouette approaching from behind. I jump with a muffled screech as a hand wraps around my throat and begins to ever so slightly squeeze. After a brief moment of panic, I register the familiar callused hand from earlier today and relax into his hold.

My body sways from the lack of blood flow, and just as the room starts to close in on itself, he releases his hold allowing the oxygen to flow back into my body, giving me an intoxicating high. Scooping me up in his arms, he carries me into a private room and over to a leather chaise and gently places me down. Looking around, I take in the bloodred velvet-like walls adorned with shelves and hooks, filled with various objects; some new to my inexperienced mind while others look as familiar like the anal plug Ramsay used and my own personal dildo. Below the shelves, hang different types of rope and an array of whips that make me clench in anticipation of what they would feel like.

Squatting in front of me, he starts to undo my stilettos, but when I pull my foot away to help, he freezes and raises his gaze until his golden orbs are locked with mine. "I'm going to let that indiscretion slide since we haven't discussed my rules, but hear me now. When you are under my command, you will do everything I say and only respond with 'sir.' If we reach a point that crosses your hard limit, you tell me your safe word, and we will stop immediately. I do not stand for disobedience, so the punishment will be dealt with immediately. Are we in agreement?"

Before I can stop myself, I start to pout. My time with Daddy was never like this. Ramsay was gentle and caring, asserting his dominance over me in a protective way, all while having control of the situation. Here I feel like I have no say except for when I refuse to do something. Breath, Royal, this is a time to learn, and remember, there's no guarantee you'll see Ramsay ever again.

"Why are you pouting? Isn't this what you want? You can leave now, and there will be no hard feelings." Even as he watches me with a predatory gaze, a flash of sincerity crossed his eyes.

"No. No, sir, I don't want to leave; this is just all new to me, and I mean, we haven't even introduced ourselves."

Sitting back, he tilts his head and lets out a sigh. Nodding his head, he slips off my other heel and sits on the chaise beside me. "My name is Sabien. I didn't know you were new by the way you handled our interaction at the diner, so forgive me . . ."

"Royal, my name is Royal. Nice to meet you. I can't promise I'll be perfect, but I'll do my best to make you happy."

"Mm-hmm, I knew you were like a goddess. Now, are you ready to play?" Giving him a coy smile, I dip my chin and nod my head. "Good, now tell me, what is your safe word? It can be anything you wish."

A million words jumble in my head, but one in particular sticks out. "London . . . sir." Satisfied, he begins to question me on my hard limits and the things I've tried, which isn't much. Spanking was Ramsay's thing, and with his desire to work me slowly, he only got to a small butt plug, which was a perfect mix of pleasure and pain.

Rising from the chaise, he moves to stand in front of me with his hands laced together behind his back and begins to trail his hungry eyes along my sun-kissed skin. Each inch that they devour, the more I feel irrevocably bare, leaving everything exposed from my aching pussy to my deeply confused soul grasping at strings to find itself.

"I want you to stand with your eyes on the ground. Don't move and don't talk." With my bottom lip dragged between my teeth, I rise from the leather chaise and stand where he points to on the ground. Complying to his command, I look down at my freshly manicured toes and brace for the unknown.

Sabien's black dress shoes disappear from my line of sight, putting me on high alert, and without thinking, I turn my head to follow his silent steps. When his hand slides from a clear glass plug down to a white leather flog-ger, I realize I messed up. Inwardly cursing myself, I quickly return my gaze to its intended spot and prepare for the spanking that's about to happen, not that I'm complaining, of course.

When nothing happens, I visibly relax, and just as I do, the bite of leather against my curved ass makes me jump. Just as quick as the searing pain registers, it changes into a delicious warmth that travels directly to my core. The sample of pain that he delivered has me wanting to drop to my knees and beg for more, for there is nothing sweeter than feeling the warmth radiating on my ass that has been thoroughly welted.

Through heavy lids, I see Sabien return to his position in front of my feet, and dangling in front of him is the deliverer of my pleasure. Reaching out, he places a finger under my chin and lifts, giving me the perfect opportunity to soak in his dominant attitude, from his crisp denim jeans that ride on his hips to his black button-up shirt that accentuates his defined arms. There's something about his rolled-up sleeves that draws my attention to the flex of his muscles, which makes the ink that saturates his skin come alive. "Look at me, pet."

Though his voice is soft, the command behind his words is evident. Lifting my gaze, I lock eyes with him and wait for whatever punishment I deserve. Slowly, his fingers trail over my chin and glide across my full lips, coaxing them to part under the gentle ministrations. I nearly think he's forgiven me of my discretion until a sinister grin crosses his face.

MY CORE TIGHTENS at the mere thought of all the things he can do to me in this room, and everything my fragile mind can think of only drives my desire higher. "I'm sorry, sir, for misbehaving. I will take any punishment . . ." My words are silenced as he shoves two of his fingers into my mouth and presses down on my tongue so I can't speak.

Instinctively, I wrap my lips around his fingers and begin to suck as if it's his cock. My tongue slides against his digits, causing an explosion of salt to erupt on my taste buds, which fills my mouth with saliva. Through my lashes, I see something cross Sabien's eyes as they become heavy with desire, but with a blink, it's gone. A need that I only felt while with Daddy hits me full force, filling me with the desire to please Sabien and be his perfect pet.

Closing my eyes, I sink into the fullness of his thick digits filling my mouth, but as soon as I find a rhythm, he pulls them out and smears his drenched fingers over my cheek, and utters, "You're fucking filthy, you know that?"

"Yes, sir." My response is nearly a purr as I lean into his fingers.

Smirking, he pulls his hand away and reaches around to give my ass a pop. "Go kneel on the chaise and lay your head flat on the bench." Not hesitating, I turn on my heels and crawl onto the chaise and slide on my knees until my head is resting on the pillow.

"Naughty, naughty. You must like to be punished, pet. Don't move from that spot and take the punishment you deserve." The silkiness of his voice caresses down my spine and slides into my aching pussy, making my channel clench. "Deviant little whore, I see. Do you know why you're getting punished, pet?

"Yes, sir."

"Tell me why."

"Because I couldn't take my eyes off of you when you told me to stare at the ground."

"What else, pet?"

My mind stutters at his question, and I quickly go over everything he said to me. Not able to think of anything, I hesitantly reply, "I . . . I don't know, sir."

"Hmm. Well, let me show you." Sabien steps so his crotch is directly in my face, and bulging against the distressed denim is an impressive outline of his hard cock. I watch through hooded eyes as his hand reaches out toward my face, but when it lands on the pillow below my face, it hits me. It seems like I can't do the simplest things.

The pillow is yanked from underneath me, making my face fall onto the cool leather. Not wanting to break the rules any further, I resist the urge to adjust to the position. My hand twitches as I watch Sabien's cock pulse through the bulging outline of his jeans, causing me to fight the inner battle to reach out and begin to stroke him. As he steps away, I let out a puff of air in relief but instantly regret it when I hear him tsking me.

Besides the shuffling feet and sounds of things being moved around, the room is completely silent, which only makes my anticipation grow. It's like swimming in the pitch-black ocean with no way to see what lays below, leaving you with the trust you have in whatever god you believe in. Trust—the only thing that matters between a Dom and their Sub.

With Sabien out of my line of sight, I'm not able to see him approaching, so when his thick fingers trail along the seam of my thong, I let out a yip that quickly turns into a purr. As he runs his fingers along the delicate material, he begins to slowly push it to the side, leaving my puckering rosebud and aching cunt fully exposed. The pop of a top is the only warning I get before chilled lube trickles down my crack, causing goosebumps to erupt over my arms and down my spine.

"Have you ever had anyone anally, pet?"

"Yes, sir, once." That time was with Ramsay, and even with me nervous, he coddled and praised me the whole way through it. The second his thick cock popped through the strangulating band, euphoric sensations overwhelmed me. Just thinking about my time with him sends a jolt of need straight to my core, drenching my pussy even further.

"This may hurt then, just relax and allow the plug to slip inside of you. If it becomes too much, you know what to do." As Sabien talks, he begins to run his finger over my slick hole, and as his last word slips past his lips, he slides his thick digit all the way in so that

his knuckles bounce against my ass. With every pump, I sink further into the sensations, letting them overtake me. I'm so steeped in the pleasure that when he withdraws his digit, I whimper.

Smack!

Sweet burning and nips of pain spread over the whole expanse of my ass, making my pussy convulse and spasm as a small orgasm erupts. The warmth is quickly replaced by an icelike bulb that begins to press against my tight ring. More lube is applied to where the connection is, and as soon as it's coated, the pressure increases. Though the sting of the stretch blends with the pain from the flogger, it feels different, almost to where it's uncomfortable.

As the pressure continues to increase, I begin to whimper. The sting is now fire and almost unbearable. Instinctively, my hips begin to swivel to escape the onslaught, but when Sabien drapes across my back to hold me still, I go against my urge to please him and say, "Sir, it hurts too much, please."

"Its almost there, pet, just bear down and relax, it's about to slide in the rest of the way. Be a good pet for your master." Even though the pain is urging me to say no, I shove it aside and do as he says. The second I press down, Sabien presses the plug harder, making it pop into place. As soon as my ring is allowed to return to a smaller state, the most sinful feeling overtakes me, leaving me shook and out of breath.

Smack!

Smack!

Smack!

Each strike lands in a different direction, and each one is harder than the last. At the last one, I'm in tears, but not from pain, no the tears that stream from my eyes are from complete joy. I've been dreaming nonstop of the feeling of being spanked and how proud I feel when I can't even sit the next day. Being on the edge of pleasure and pain is addicting, and it's a drug I never want to give up.

I want to beg for more, but the sound of a zipper stops me. It's been nearly two weeks since I've had a real cock filling me, and judging by his outline, I'm in for a treat.

Movement on the bench causes my knees to slip, which lowers me a little, but judging by

the head pressing into the entrance of my pussy, I'm at the perfect height. There's no prep this time; instead, Sabien slides into me, filling me to the brim. With the plug inserted into place and the girth on his cock, I'm overly stuffed. Not giving me a chance to adjust to his member, he begins to thrust . . . much harder and faster than I've ever experienced. Though my pussy is gushing and quivering around his cock, I can't stop a niggling feeling from the back of my mind. Brushing the thought to the side, I focus back on Sabien and his ferocious movements that are quickly bringing me closer to the edge.

With one hand on my hip, Sabien reaches around and begins to rub my engorged clit, making me nearly buck him off at the trifecta of sensations. "Be a good pet and come for me. Let me feel your tight pussy clench my dick."

The rubber band that's holding me together snaps at his command, sending me soaring through a kaleidoscope of emotions. My core grasps at his cock, not wanting to let it go and every muscle in my body spasms, making me collapse onto the bench. Behind me, Sabien begins to grunt, and instead of coating my core with his seed, he slides out of my quivering channel and spills it across my ass and back.

Unlike my time with Ramsey, Sabien doesn't collapse down with me or praise me for being his perfect little girl, he doesn't run his fingers through my thick locks as he whispers how beautiful I am, and most importantly, he doesn't make me feel like he truly cared if we were both satisfied with our physical connection. Not wanting to get in trouble, I keep my questions to myself and remain flat on the leather couch, even as Sabien grips the plug and begins to remove it. Biting my lip, I fight to keep the scream of pain locked away, and as soon as it's removed, I sigh the biggest breath of relief.

After a few more minutes, he has me cleaned up, and we are both dressed. With my hand on the door to leave our room, I look over my shoulder and call back to Sabien, who is still adjusting his jeans, "Thank you, sir, for taking care of my needs." No matter the conflicting emotions surging through me, I know one thing for sure, I want to be a good girl.

THE REST of my trip to France was spent exploring Paris and acting like a normal tourist who overeats new food and takes pictures of every site and attraction around. But by the time my week was over, I was ready to move on. Aside from sightseeing, I returned back to the club and spent more time with Sabien, and each time we spent together, the harsher he became. By the fourth night, he pressed me to my limit, and I had to use my safe-word. In an instant, his Dom personality disappeared, and a caring side of him that I never saw before appeared.

After telling Ramsay what happened, he made it his mission to cheer me up with pictures from his business trip and all the historical sites he stopped at. At times I felt like he was going out of his way to send me snapshots of certain places that I told him I was dying to see. Even with all the humorous messages, he still found a way of making me hotter than sin, and though thousands of miles separate us, he still asserted his dominance.

We may have only met just over three weeks ago, but our chemistry is one of a

long-term relationship, and little does he know, but his name on my phone is Daddy. He always tells me I'm his little brat and how much he enjoyed tanning my hide.

I've nearly come to the point of begging him to join me here at my new destination, but that would be foolish. The man has a career and will most likely forget about me in no time.

Brushing the thoughts away, I turn down Wangfujing, a bustling street in Beijing full of pedestrians, street food, and shops. The exotic smells immediately hit me, making my stomach growl, reminding me that the last decent meal I had was two nights ago. I promised Ramsay I would eat yesterday, but when I told him I only had clear vegetable soup, he swore that when he sees me again to expect to receive punishment. I scoff at the thought since when will more than likely be in Neverland.

As if sensing my wandering thoughts, my phone dings with a message from Daddy. I can't help but smirk at his name popping up on my screen. I wonder what my mother would think . . . actually, I take that back, it's none of her business. When I swipe the message open, I nearly drop my phone from what I see. Spinning around, I come face to face with the man who's been haunting my dreams.

"Ramsay, what are you doing here? I thought you had a flight to Canada?" I can't help but stare—his light-blue dress shirt accentuates his biceps and his trimmed waistline and his gray slacks mold against his toned thighs. You would think that having the two top buttons undone would make him look unattractive with his sparse chest hair hanging out, except for him, it's the complete opposite. Under the opulent reflections from the mosaic windows, the fine hair shimmers only adding to his panty-dropping appearance.

With his burning oceanic-blue eyes locked on me, he dips his chin and begins to close the distance between us. His movement is like a stealthy lion on the prowl for his next meal, and I'm the prey. Under his intense gaze, I can't help but feel completely nude, even standing in the busy street with people bustling around us. Instinctively, my arms wrap around my midsection to cover myself as much as possible, but as soon as I do, Ramsay frowns, and I realize what I did.

Our week together was one I will never forget, so how I forgot one of his very basic rules baffles me. I can try to blame it on the fact I'm new to his lifestyle or maybe the fact I never thought I would see him again. But deep inside, I know that's not the truth. I remember his rules, I just miss the way his hand stings when he delivers the delicious spanking that leaves my ass tingling and my core aching. His words echo in my mind as if he is whispering them right now and as they playback, I slowly lower my arms, leaving myself exposed to his carnivorous glare.

Stopping so that we're nearly toe to toe, he reaches out and places a finger under my chin, and with the silkiest voice I've ever heard, he utters, "There's my little princess. I'm not sure what spell you've placed on me, but I can't get you out of my head."

"I thought I would never see you again. Why didn't you let me know you were coming here? I coulda met . . ." My flustered questions are muted as Ramsay's finger presses against my lips, causing me to pout. Stepping back, I cross my arms over my chest and stomp my foot. "Don't shush me. I hate surprises, and now I gotta cancel my plans on slumming it at the hotel."

With a twitch of his jaw, Ramsay cocks his head to the side and closes the distance between us once again. "Now, princess, don't make me punish you right here in the middle of the road. You know I prefer to keep our relations private, but I will gladly leave prints on your pretty cheeks in front of everyone."

"I just don't get it . . . what did I do to deserve you? No one in their right mind would fly to another country for no reason." Like my ex-husband always told me, I'm just a pretty trophy wife, and no one would waste their time on me. I may exude an abundance of confidence, but the lingering wounds from that rat bastard are still healing, and somehow, Ramsay knows which scabs to rip off, leaving me exposed.

"I didn't fly into a different country for no reason. So,

Forgetting about the people weaving around us, I jump and wrap myself around Ramsay and close my mouth over his. Finally, back in his embrace, I feel complete, and as if everything I will ever need is here in my arms. , all the love and trust, and my urge to be his bratty princess for as long as he'll have me.

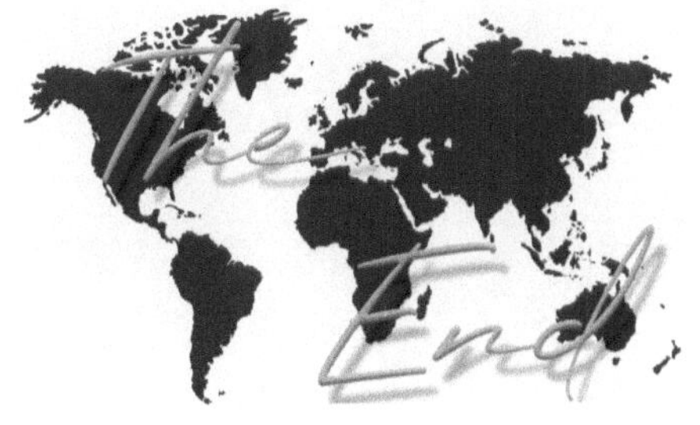
The End

Yo.

I'm Darcy Ray & I write books.

I'm a full-time RN, fur baby mama, and take care of my pain in the ass husband. I've been married to my soulmate since February of 2011 and together we have three fur babies and three fish. My favorite smells are chlorine and banana boat tanning oil, and I have a tendency to get super burnt when at the beach. When I'm not writing, I'm playing PC games or heading to the closest springs to tube down the rivers. I guess you can say I'm a Florida girl for life.

Stay Salty xoxo

Amazon: amazon.com/author/darcyray
Fan Group: https://www.facebook.com/groups/darcysdarlings
Author Page: https://www.facebook.com/authordray/
Goodreads: https://www.goodreads.com/Darcy_Ray
BookBub: https://www.bookbub.com/profile/darcy-ray
Instagram: https://www.instagram.com/darcy_ray_author/
Twitter: http://twitter.com/AuthorDarcyRay
Website/Newsletter: https://www.darcyrayauthor.com/